Ike Matthews

Full Revelations of a Professional Rat-Catcher

After 25 Years Experience

Ike Matthews

Full Revelations of a Professional Rat-Catcher
After 25 Years Experience

ISBN/EAN: 9783337337773

Printed in Europe, USA, Canada, Australia, Japan

Cover: Foto ©Andreas Hilbeck / pixelio.de

More available books at **www.hansebooks.com**

FULL REVELATIONS

OF A

Professional Rat-catcher,

After 25 Years' Experience.

BY

IKE MATTHEWS.

INTRODUCTION.

IN placing before my readers in the following pages the results of my twenty-five years' experience of Rat-catching, Ferreting, &c., I may say that I have always done my best to accomplish every task that I have undertaken, and I have in consequence received excellent testimonials from many corporations, railway companies, and merchants. I have not only made it my study to discover the different and the best methods of catching Rats, but I have also taken great interest in watching their ways and habits, and I come to the conclusion that there is no sure way of completely exterminating the Rodents, especially in large towns. If I have in this work referred more particularly to Rat-catching in Manchester that is only because my experience, although extending over a much wider area, has been chiefly in that city, but the methods I describe are equally applicable to all large towns.

Yours truly,
IKE MATTHEWS.

PROFESSIONAL RAT-CATCHER,
    PENDLETON,
        MANCHESTER.

The Revelations of a Rat-catcher.

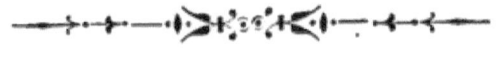

PART I.

HOW TO CLEAR RATS FROM WAREHOUSES, OFFICES, STOREROOMS, &c.

IN the first place my advice is—never poison Rats in any enclosed buildings whatever. Why? Simply because the Rats that you poison are Drain Rats, or what you call Black Rats, and you can depend upon it that the Rats that you poison will not get back into the drains, but die under the floor between the laths and plaster, and the consequence is that in a few days the stench that will arise will be most obnoxious. And there is nothing more injurious than the smell of a decomposed Rat.

Having had a long experience in Manchester I am quite sure of this. As an instance, I remember a private house where I was engaged catching Rats under a floor with ferrets. I went as far as possible on my belly under the floor with two candles in my hands, and I saw the ferret kill a large bitch Rat, about six yards from me against a wall, where neither the dog nor myself could get at it. I finished the job and made out my bill for my services, but in about two or three weeks after they again sent for me, declaring they could not stay in the sitting-room on account of the smell that arose from beneath the flooring boards. They had in consequence to send for a joiner; and as I knew the exact spot where the Rat was killed I ordered him to take up the floor boards just where the dead Rat lay, and the stench that arose from the decomposed Rodent was bad in the extreme. I disinfected the place, and I was never sent for again. This was under a cold floor, and it is much worse where there is any heat.

Now to deal with the different methods of catching Rats. The best way, in my opinion, is TRAPPING THEM WITH STEEL SPRING TRAPS. Whenever you are trapping, never on any consideration put bait on the traps; always put traps in their runs, but you will find Rats are so cunning that in time, after a few have been caught, they will jump over the traps, and then you must try another way. A good one is the following, viz.:—Get a bag of fine, clean sawdust, and mix with it about one-sixth its weight of oatmeal. Obtain the sawdust fresh from under the saw, without bits of stick in, as these would be liable to get into the teeth of the trap and stop them from closing. Where you see the runs put a handful in say about 30 different places, every night, just dropping the sawdust and meal out of your hands in little heaps. That means 30 different heaps. Do this for four nights, and you will see each morning that the sawdust is all spread about. Now for four more nights you must bury a set trap under every heap of sawdust. Thus you will have 30 traps, on each of which there is a square centre plate; you must level the sawdust over the plate with a bit of stick, and set each trap as fine as you can on the catch spring, so that the weight of a mouse would set it off. They will play in the sawdust as usual, and you will have Rats in almost every trap. You will find that this plan will capture a great many of the Rodents. I have trapped as many as 114 in one night in this way.

In time, however, the Rats will cease to go near sawdust. Then you must procure a bag of fine soot from any chimney sweep, and you will find that they will go at the soot just as keen as they did in the first instance at the sawdust. When they get tired of soot (which they will in time) you must procure some soft tissue paper and cut it fine, and use that in the same way as the sawdust and the soot. You can also use light chaff or hay seeds with the like result.

I must not omit to tell my readers to always trap Rats in the night, and to go very quietly about it, for if you make much noise they will give over feeding. You must not go about with too big a light whilst trapping. You should stay at the building from dark until midnight, and every time a Rat is caught in the trap you should go with a bull's eye lamp, take it out of the trap or kill it, and then set the trap again, as you have the chance of another Rat in the same trap. From experience I can say that you need not stay in any place after 12 o'clock at night, as I think that the first feed is the best, and that the first three hours are worth all the other part of the night. You can go home at 12 o'clock, and be sure to be in the place by 6 or 7 a.m., for many a Rat caught in the trap by the front leg will, if it gets time, eat off its leg and get away again, and they are very cunning to catch afterwards.

NEVER HAVE YOUR TRAPS SET IN THE DAYTIME.

Handle them as little as possible. Always catch as many Rats as you can in your buildings in January and February, as they begin to breed in March, and every bitch Rat means, on the average, eight more. Also get as much ferreting done as possible before breeding time, for a young Rat can get into the ends of the joisting under a floor, where a ferret cannot get near it, and the consequence is that a ferret is unable to cope with its task. The best thing I can advise for clearing young Rats is a good cat, one that must not be handled nor made a pet of, but allowed to live in almost a wild state. A good cat can do as much, in my opinion, in one night, when Rats are breeding, as two ferrets can do in a day, especially in a building where there are cavity walls, as it is impossible for a ferret to follow a Rat in such walls.

This is all the information I am able to give on the trapping of Rats—a method I have proved by 25 years' experience to excel all others. Still another way of clearing the pests is as follows :—The majority of Rats are Black, or what we call Drain Rats; if they are in a building they will in most cases come from a water-closet. Sometimes you will see from the drain pipes in the water-closet, say, a six-inch pipe fitted into a nine-inch pipe, and the joint covered round with clay, through which the Rats eat and scratch and get into the building in great numbers in the night, but most of them return into the drains during the day. Now, if it is the breeding season (about eight months out of the twelve) they will do much damage to silk, cotton, leather, lace, and, in fact, all other light goods. And one would be surprised to see the quantity of cloth, paper, &c., they will procure for their nests whilst breeding.

The way to get clear of these is to go in the day with two or three ferrets and leave the drain pipe open. Ferret them all back into the drain; don't put a net over the drain for fear you might miss one or two. If they got back into the building they would be hard to catch, as they would not face the net again. Then, after ferreting, make the drain good, and if there be an odd Rat or two left in the building you will get them in a few nights by baiting the trap.

There is another way of catching the Brown Rat which breeds under the floor in large buildings where there are no drains. They are very awkward to catch. Always have a trap or two set, but do not set them where they feed; place them in their runs. But there are other methods for other Rat-infested places. For instance, take a restaurant, where they feed in the cooking kitchen; we will suppose they have eaten four holes through either floor or skirting boards. The best way to catch these—however many holes they have leading into the kitchen—is to block up (with tin or similar material) all the holes with the exception of one, and let them use that one for two nights. Then put a plateful of good food, such as oatmeal and oil of aniseed, as far from the hole as you can in the same kitchen; then run a small train of meal and aniseed from the hole to the plate. Next drive two six-inch nails in the wall, with a long piece of string tied to the nail heads. Put on these nails a brick or piece of board right above the hole 2in. up the wall. Be sure the nails are quite loose in the wall over the hole, and leave in that position for two nights, so that the Rats will get used to it. On the night that you are going to catch them, before leaving the place carry the string from the nail heads to the door or window; let the door or window be closed within an inch, with the end of the string outside. After the place has been quiet for thirty minutes return to the door or window very quietly, and you will hear the Rats feeding. Pull the string, the loose nails come out of the wall and the brick or board drops over the hole. You can then go in, close the door, turn up the gas and catch or kill them at your leisure, as they cannot get back again.

By this method I may mention that I have caught a great number of Rats, and it is quite possible to clear a place in this manner: that is, if they do not come out of the drains. I have caught upwards of 103 in six nights in this way. The best time to catch Rats in any building is always at night, and always about half-an-hour after the place has been closed, as Rats are generally more adventurous to come for their first feed. Always go about as quietly as possible.

In some of the very old Manchester buildings that were built in the days before drain plans had to be submitted to the corporation, one finds under the cellar floors old-fashioned brick and flag drains (better known as "spit" drains), that were left in when the place was built. Once the Rats get in these disused drains all the professional Rat-catchers in England could not clear them without pulling the building down. The Rats have, by some means, got out of the main sewer, probably by the bursting of a sewer into one of these disused dry brick drains. It is then impossible to get underground to see where they have got into the dry drain, and the only thing that can be done in a case of this sort is to engage a professional Rat-catcher occasionally, and keep two or three good cats to keep the Rats down. These places as a rule are more plagued with them when it is very wet weather and there are floods running. This is the best time to catch them, as they are all under the floor of the building, and are very easy to catch in the night with the traps.

As a rule the Black or Drain Rats feed only in the night, very rarely in the day, as they are of a dirty nature, and prefer being in the drains. In my opinion the Black Rat is more vicious than the Brown.

There is another Rat I call the Red Rat, which is akin to the Brown Rat. You will always catch these at a tannery, or about kennels, where hounds are kept, and they generally feed on horseflesh or offal. Red Rats are the "gameist" Rats I know, for whatever kind of Rats are put into the store cage, these Red Rats kill them the first night they are left quiet.

I may describe another mode of catching Rats. In any Rat-overrun warehouse, store-room, or cellar, where there is a deal of rubbish such as packing cases, wrappers, waste paper, &c., throw a lot of food, say oatmeal or soaked bread, carelessly amongst the cases or rubbish and let the Rats have a full week's feeding at their leisure, and then if you know the holes round the floor wherefrom they come, go in some night as quick as possible, turn up the lights, run to the three or four holes, and block them up with pieces of rag, &c. Now as all the Rats will not run out of the packing cases or waste paper, but will hide amongst the same, this is the time to take a good terrier dog or two with you, and to have a bit of sport. Let one dog hunt among the cases, &c., and hold the other, for the Rats will soon make for the holes, but the rags preventing their escape you will catch and kill a great many by this means.

It should be stated here that as Rats are very cunning, it takes a lot of study, dodging, and experience to be able to rid them entirely. When you are feeding Rats anywhere, never feed them with other than soft stuff, which you can squeeze through your fingers, for if you feed them with anything lumpy, they will carry pieces into their holes and eat at their leisure.

FERRETING.

Ferreting is a very good plan for destroying Rats in cottage houses, stables, hotels, &c., as it can be done in the day, but in buildings, say five ro six storeys high you cannot ferret very well as you cannot tell where to set your nets. The only way to ferret a large building is to ferret one floor at once, and always start at the top storey first. The majority of floors are laths and plaster. This is what the Rat likes, especially the Brown Rat, and there are more nests found in these places than anywhere else. To ferret thoroughly in such places you will require to have a board up at each end of the floor : the two end boards that run crossways with the joist; then you must have a man to put the ferret in at one end, and ferret one joist at a time; have a net set at the other end. The best way at the catching end is to have a long sheet net about a yard wide, and the full length of the boards that are up, for sometimes under the boards the Rats can get out of one joist into another, and if you use the long net you can catch them whichever joist they bolt at.

Now we will suppose you are ferreting a seven-storey building, which might occupy three or four days. If you have ferreted two stories the first day, during the night the Rats that have not been ferreted on the lower stories may get back again to the top storey.

How to prevent .this happening I will give you a plan of my own, which I don't think any Rat-catcher but myself has ever employed. The course of action—a rather expensive one I admit—is the following : While you have the boards up you must go to the druggist and get two shillings' worth of cayenne pepper, and put it into a pepper duster. Scatter the cayenne along the boards and joist where you have had the long sheet net, and also along the other end of the joist where you put the ferrets in, and you will find that under no consideration will Rats face the cayenne pepper. Cayenne is alright for any dry place and will last a long time, but it will not do in any water closets or any damp places, as dampness takes all the nature out of the cayenne.

After ferreting in any kind of building, always go carefully round the outside, and see that there are no broken air grids, or broken cellar windows, as these are likely ways that the Rats get into the building at first. When ferreting always be careful how you set your nets, and be extremely quick on the Rats when they bolt, for sometimes if they get back they will face the ferret before they will bolt again; then the ferrets kill them under the floors, and this as in the case of poisoning them is liable to cause an abominable smell, more especially where heat is near.

In the whole of my experience of Rat-catching, which is a lengthy one, I never gave a guarantee to clear a place completely, in Manchester or any other town where so many large buildings are so close together. And let me show the reason for this. Take Cannon

Street, Manchester, as an illustration. Here are six or eight different firms in one block of buildings. Now, suppose four of these firms are suffering from the damage the Rats are doing. Well, one or two of these firms may go to the expense of having the Rats cleared away. But between the two buildings there may be a hardware business or ironmonger's shop, where Rats cannot do any harm to their goods. The owners of these shops will not go to the expense of having Rats caught, nor will they let us go into their shops at midnight; therefore the result is the Rat-catcher in his trapping and ferretting is limited to these two places, and all he can do is to catch some and drive the rest into the hardware shop. When under the floors in such places one finds there has been so many alterations made at different times that one joist may be a foot or six inches below the other, and when the Rats are completely driven out of these places it would require joiners and bricksetters to work for weeks under the floors to stop the Rats returning. And most firms will not go to this expense. I only give my readers this as an illustration of what has often happened with me, and to show why I never guarantee to clear Rats completely in large towns. If they are in a private house, stable, greenhouse, or any block of houses, of say five or six, I might then, after looking through, give a guarantee to clear them completely.

These are the fullest details I can give you, and if you will put any of the ways I have mentioned into practice you will find that they are all successful, especially the covering of traps. I can give you just one more instance in Manchester, where I was engaged. The workpeople had been tormenting the Rats with traps, not knowing how to set them. They sent for me, and on my looking round the place I knew there was a lot of Rats. I submitted my price to do the job, and when I went down one night with 40 traps, dog, and two ferrets I thought I should catch 20 or 30 Rats, but I found that they had plagued them so much with their attempted trapping that I only caught three in the whole night. This place belonged to a limited company, and when I went before the committee the next morning they were not satisfied. I told them that their own workpeople had tormented the Rats so much with traps that the Rats would not go near one. I then told the committee that I would still stick to my terms, but I would leave the job over for a fortnight. Now during that fortnight I went down a good many times, and laid the sawdust as I have already described, and thus got the Rats used to it. The first night that I went catching I took with me 33 traps. I had them all set by 8-30 p.m., and by 12-30 a.m. I had trapped 45 Rats; the next night 31 Rats; and before I completed the job, with the trapping and the other ways that I have mentioned, I caught 183 Rats! This I give merely as an illustration to show the necessity of engaging an experienced man to catch Rats—that is, if you want them caught. And to confirm the statements above, I shall be most happy to supply privately the name and place of the firm, and also to give a personal interview if necessary.

And now a word or two respecting the different ways in which Rat-catchers are treated. Many people think that a Rat-catcher is favoured if they give him permission to catch Rats on their farms or round the banks of their corn or wheat fields. Well, on some occasions I grant this may be a favour, for I have seen when I have had an order in hand for about 10 dozen Rats, and have had only a day or two in which to get them. Such are the only times and circumstances when a Rat-catcher gives his services gratis, and simply because he wants the live Rats. Most farmers will send you word when they are

c

threshing their corn, and then the value of the Rats are worth the day's work to the Rat-catcher.

This is all right as far as it goes, but when one comes to consider the yearly expenses of the Rat-catcher it will be found that they are very heavy. Now, first of all it will cost, at the least, £5 annually for the wear and tear of traps alone, then there is the wear and tear of nets; two dog licences; always three or four ferrets to keep (and ferrets are often lost down drains or killed by Rats); also sundry other expenses, such as store cages, &c. Then, again, the Rat-catcher always has to pay a man to help him.

I don't call Rat-catching a trade only: I maintain that it is a profession, and one that requires much learning and courage. I have found this out when I have been under a warehouse floor, where a lot of Rats were in the traps, and I could not get one man out of 50 to come under the floor and hold the candle for me, not to mention helping me to take the live Rats out of the traps. I just relate this because at some places where we go and where we catch perhaps 30 Rats, the first thing they say when the bill is presented is "Why, you have got 15s. worth of live Rats!" They don't think of the damage 30 Rats can do to fancy goods, nor do they consider the evil smells that men have to tolerate under the floors or from the bad drains.

I could relate many interesting anecdotes of what I have seen and heard about Rats, but I fear its perusal might take up too much of my readers' time. There is, however, one thing I will mention. I dare say you have heard of Rats running about in "swarms" in the night. Do not believe it. In my whole experience I have never been so fortunate as to meet a "swarm" of these, when I have had an empty cage on my back, and an order for 12 dozen live Rats at 5s. per dozen. When trapping at farms on a moonlight night I have seen a train of Rats almost in single file going from a barn to a pit or brook to drink, and then I have simply run a long net all along the barn very quickly, sent my dog round the pit and caught all the Rats in the net when they ran back to get in the barn. For in these places you must be as cunning as the Rats to catch them. The quickest way for a farmer to get rid of Rats is to run a long trail of good oatmeal outside his barn doors, and shoot them on a moonlight night. I have seen 11 killed at a shot in this way. They will stop eating the oatmeal because they cannot carry it away. At farms or out-houses you might

poison Rats round a pit or along brook sides
where they go to drink, although I don't believe
in poisoning, as one never knows where it ends
—the Rats being likely to carry the poisoned
food about, and then dogs, hens, pigs, pigeons,
&c., may pick it up.

There may be a few more ways of catching
Rats than I have enumerated, but I think I
have given the best ways in detail. Some
people think that to use

THE MONGOOSE

is very good, but I think that the mongoose is
no better than a good fox terrier dog or a good
cat, the only advantage in the mongoose being
that all the Rats it kills it will bring back dead
to its habitation, and that stops the dead
Rats from smelling under the floors. I think
that the mongoose is not half so sly or sharp
as a good cat, and a mongoose, moreover, has
to be taught how to kill a Rat (just the same
as a dog). I am fortunate in having actually
seen a mongoose and a Rat put alive in a tub
together, and the mongoose would not even
look at the Rat. And I maintain that the
mongoose cannot compare with the ferret
anytime, for the simple reason that a small
ferret can get anywhere that a Rat can,
whilst the mongoose must wait until the Rat
comes out to feed. For instance, if a board

of a floor be left up for a mongoose to get under the floor, it can only get into one of the joists; but a ferret can follow a Rat wherever it goes. Then again, the Rats can smell a mongoose even more strongly than they can smell a cat. So these facts prevent my recommending a mongoose on any account. I have also heard of people experimenting with different sorts of

DRUGS AND CHEMICALS

for enticing Rats out of their holes. I hope none of my readers will be attracted with this device. I hold that there is nothing that will tempt a Rat from its hole like hunger. The nearest approach that I have found to entice the Rodent out of its hole is oil of aniseed or oil of rhodium, but the latter is expensive. I can rely best on oil of aniseed, because I have often successfully tried it in experiment upon the plate of a set trap. I have placed only three or four drops of oil of aniseed upon the plate of a set trap without bait, and often the trap has closed and trapped the Rat by the nose; so that it will be seen that the Rat must have been licking the plate, or it could not be caught in that manner. I have also frequently noticed when I have set, say, 20 traps covered with meal and sawdust mixed, that if I have put only two drops of oil of aniseed on half the traps I should find next morning on looking at the traps that most Rats are in those in which I had placed the aniseed. I think that oil of rhodium and oil of aniseed are very good to drop on the traps after setting, or to mix with the stuff with which the traps are covered.

There is also another way of bolting Rats. Sometimes when the ferret is put under a boarded floor, all the Rats will run together and pack themselves in a heap at the end of a joist. When the Rats pack themselves on each other thus, the ferret on reaching them will tackle only one at a time. You can always tell when this happens by the ferret working a long time and bolting no Rats. Now, immediately you notice this, put your mouth near the hole where you have put the ferrets in, and make a squealing noise with your mouth to imitate a squealing Rat. This causes the heap of Rats at the end of the joist to disperse through fear, and when they get running about they will bolt into the net. Many times I have not had a bolt for half-an-hour and when I have squealed at the hole I have had four or five Rats in the nets at once.

These are some of the methods of clearing Rats from various places, and from experience I think they excel all others.

PART II

HOW TO KEEP AND WORK FERRETS.

THE first necessity in ferret-keeping is that they shall be kept in hutches or "cotes," as they are commonly called. Care must always be taken to have their places well swilled with carbolic water, and then allowed to thoroughly dry before whitewashing the inside, which is also essential to keep them healthy. This should be done at least four times a year. Always have your hutches leaning from the wall, so that wet or refuse will not lodge, for when the bottom of a hutch is always wet it is liable to give the ferrets a disease called foot rot, which is very frequent where ferrets are neglected. Always keep the feeding part of the hutch well covered with sawdust.

In feeding ferrets for the purpose of Rat-catching, never do so before going out with them; I think it is quite sufficient to feed them every 24 hours. If you feed them oftener they are liable to get too fat, and also lazy and unwilling to work as they should. The best food you can give them is bread and

milk, and occasionally a little raw liver. Mix
the bread and milk with a little hot water, stir
well with a spoon or squeeze through your
fingers, so that the ferrets will have to eat it
where you feed them; if not they will carry
the large pieces of bread that are wet into the
corners of the sleeping place, which would
soon cause that part of the hutch to smell
very sour and become injurious to the health
of the ferret, especially where four or five
are kept together, as they are of a very
perspiring nature. Always give them plenty
of room to run about when you can; if you
don't they are likely to take cramp.

Ferrets are usually subject to distemper.
The first symptom is the ferret's neglect of
its food. When you see this you will observe
a little matter at the corner of the eyes, and
the ferret will have a slight running at the
nostrils. Immediately you see these symptoms
separate that ferret from the others, as this is,
I think, the worst disease one has to contend
with.

In the whole of my ferret-keeping experience
I have found distemper, if caught in time, can
be cured; but if it gets too far I know of no
cure for it. I have known a gamekeeper to
have dogs with the distemper, and he has not
touched his ferrets or handled them at all

during the time his dogs were bad, yet a week afterwards his ferrets caught the disease. He tried all the remedies he knew of, but in 14 days 12 hitherto good, strong, healthy ferrets died : all he had. This will show at once that the disease is very contagious. The moment you see signs of distemper coming on feed the ferret as little as possible. Give it as little to eat as will just keep life in it, for in feeding the ferret you also feed the disease. When you have kept the food from it is the time to start curing if possible. Now, from experience the first thing I recommend is to sweat the disease out of it, and I find the best way to do this is as follows :—Get an old bucket with a few one-inch holes bored in the bottom, and almost fill it with good new straw horse-droppings; put a little hay on the top of the droppings, and then put the ferret on the hay. Place or hang the bucket over a boiler or on the mantelpiece, and let the kettle steam under the bucket, say for 30 minutes, and you will find the steam and the ammonia from the droppings will together sweat the disease out of the ferret; then you can start feeding it again. Feed it with something substantial, such as the jelly from stewed cowheels; give them the jelly only, not the meat; and you will have a good result. Also give them teaspoonful of cream. This is the one and only cure for distemper.

Another disease in ferrets, especially young ones, is what I call "red mange." This starts always under the belly, and you will find that the skin becomes very red and speckled. This is easily remedied by the simple process of washing in lukewarm water and rubbing with sweet oil and black sulphur. The same mixture will answer for "foot rot" if rubbed well into the paws. The general cause of this latter disease is neglect of the ferrets and the hutches not being cleaned out regularly.

I think the best bedding for ferrets is good oat straw, fresh every fortnight. Throw the straw in carelessly, and the ferrets will make their own beds. When breeding ferrets never go near them more than you can help, as they are of a wild nature and liable to destroy their young. When you know a Jill or bitch ferret has young, give her a little extra good food, but don't interfere with the young ones on any account, and if you want to give her a little extra bedding put the straw in the same place as the food, and she will take it into the sleeping place herself. It is advisable not to touch the young ones for five weeks, or better still, leave them until they come out to feed themselves ; and when running about, if there be a good number, say nine or ten, in the lot, it is a good plan to remove them into a larger place for sleeping, as young ferrets are very liable to catch the red mange, which arises from too many being together and sweating very much.

WHEN WORKING FERRETS FOR RAT-CATCHING always work them unmuzzled. Make as little noise as possible, as Rats are very bad to bolt sometimes. Never grab at the ferret as it leaves the hole, nor tempt it out of the hole with a dead Rat. The best way is to let the ferret come out of its own choice, and then pick it up very quietly, for if you grab at it it is likely to become what we call a " stopper ;" and never on any account force a ferret to go into a hole.

WHEN WORKING FERRETS FOR RABBIT-SHOOTING always muzzle them. The old-fashioned style of muzzle is, I think, the best, that is, made with string. I don't approve of wire muzzles, as they are liable to catch against tree roots and bits of sharp stones, and from experience I find the ferret works much better with the string muzzle.

There is one way of working ferrets when rabbit-shooting which, if followed, I think would lead to a better day's shooting. You will often see the ferrets stick up with the rabbits. Now, in most cases the gamekeeper or his man working the ferrets will often cut open a dead rabbit and put the paunch to the burrow. I quite agree as to the desirability of this to get the ferrets out, but I say that the man using the ferrets ought never to touch the paunch, as the ferrets will not work half so well after he has the smell of the paunch on his hands.

Another bad plan is that of throwing a dead rabbit into the burrow so that the ferret will follow it out The best plan is to let the ferret get clear of the hole, and then pick it up quietly. If you will break your ferrets in in this manner you will never have any trouble with them afterwards.

When ferrets are conveyed about for the purpose of rabbiting, boxes are much better to use than bags, as the ferrets then get a better chance of resting. If bags be used you disturb the ferrets' rest and position each time you remove one. Take care to observe this and it will result in a good day's sport.

Always take your ferrets home as quickly as possible after a day's work.

Ferrets kept only for rabbit-shooting should always be fed as soon as the day's work is over, but thay must not have more food till the same time the following day. If fed in this way regularly you will find that they will work very well. It is also advisable to let them drink at a stream when they have worked about three hours.

When ferrets have been ast in a rabbit burrow, their paws may be full of down with scratching at the rabbits. Always remove this before placing them to another burrow. Each time you handle the ferret see that the muzzle is alright, and in muzzling with string great care should be taken to remove the long hair on the snout from under the string; otherwise the ferret may experience a tickling sensation, and not work so well as it should; see also that the string is tied tightly around the ferret's neck; if not it can easily pull off the muzzle with its paws.

Whenever a ferret is severely bitten by a Rat the best course to take immediately you get it home is to bathe the wound in clean luke-warm water. See that all the dirt is removed, and then apply a few drops of sweet oil to the wound. Repeat this every four hours until the wound is healed, but until then do not work the ferret lest more dirt gets into the wound. My experience proves this to be the best way to cure a ferret when it has received a severe Rat-bite.

It is also a good plan occasionally (say

once a fortnight) to skin a nice young Rat and give it to the ferret.

Suitable Dogs.

And now a word or two as to what is a good dog for waterside hunting, or working with the ferrets. I recommend a cross-bred dog, but I find that it is always better to have the pointer breed in it, whatever other breed you get, because the pointer always has the nose or scent. Pointer and Airedale would be very good, or pointer and Irish terrier. I have often noticed that pure-bred dogs are not much good for hunting in buildings or rivers. I have frequently seen a cross-bred dog stand at one side of the river, and if the wind has been in his favour he has winded his nose across the river, and I have sent him over and he has turned a Rat out, bolted it into the water, and killed it.

The best precaution to take in breaking a dog to Rat-catching and waterside hunting (especially if it be a puppy) is to never allow anybody but yourself to have anything to do with it, it being the worst thing possible to let a working dog have too many masters. Break it in to the ferrets first, and then it is a good plan to go up the river banks, with either a dead Rat or rabbit skin, letting the dog play with it for a while, and then burying it about

18 inches in the river bank; or you may pull up a clod and put it under, only you must not let the dog see where you place it. Then take the dog with you near to where the rat or skin is buried, and you will soon see that the dog knows its work. Do this a few times, and you will see that once the dog finds the dead Rat or the skin it will never forget. The younger the dog the better, the right age to break a puppy this way being about four or five months. Break it in for taking to the water at the same time. If you want a good working dog always keep it on the chain when at home, and feed it at the same time as the ferrets, but do not over-feed it; also give it one dose of castor oil or syrup of buckthorn every 14 days. I recommend this because you never know the nasty poisonous stuff that the dog gets on its stomach from the dirty brook and river sides.

Let me add that all I have written about ferrets and dogs are not given merely from hearsay, but are the facts derived 'from study and experience during 25 years of dog and ferret-keeping.

PART III.

THE HABITS OF RATS.

RATS breed very quickly. This I have often proved by visiting a given haunt for many years together. I remember an instance in point one June, when out with dog and ferrets. The dog made a set under the root of a tree. I put the ferret in and it bolted eight young Rats, nearly half grown, still suckling the bitch Rat. When the old Rat bolted my dog killed it, and whilst the dog was shaking it I found she was very heavy in young again. This, therefore, will prove how quickly Rats breed.

Another result of my observation may be of interest to my readers. After removing a lot of old rubbish when ratting I came upon a nest of just-born Rats, and, in curiosity, I cut the tails off the lot, and then put the young Rodents back, leaving the nest undisturbed. When I returned next day, I found the old Rat had carried all her young away, and, later, I found the same tailless lot in another part of the building, and, after disturbing them again, I found the following day that the bitch Rat had killed every one by eating off their heads.

This destruction of the offspring I have witnessed on more than one occasion. The old bitch Rat has always killed them in the same way by eating off their heads.

I must not forget to tell you of the young Rat's dread of the ferrets. I have often seen when the ferrets have been put in the hole the young Rats (not many days old and their eyes yet unopened) creep out of the hole. This is a proof that the smell of the ferrets has a tendency to bolt Rats, either young or old.

Old Rats are very bold whilst suckling their young. I have seen them very venturesome to get to water, and more eager for water than for food. I have often traced their runs a long way for water, and noticed that when crossing a field to get to a pit or river they never walk, but are always on the run; and in the summer, when they reach the pit, they not only drink, but often swim about. I have frequently watched them swimming on a moonlight night, but they generally go back to the buildings in the early morning, especially in the winter months.

Another habit I have often noticed. Take a farm, or any place where there are many Rats, and it will be always found that when a Rat gets very old it becomes very greyish in colour and rather scabbed, and its hair comes

D

off, mostly on the back. The healthy Rats will then drive the old Rat away, and these scabby old Rats may be caught by themselves in other parts of the buildings; and, further, I often notice that if the ferrets are bitten with these old Rats, they "take bad ways." I never put such Rats with the others nor allow my dog to kill them. I would advise any gentleman having a dog he values never to let it touch one of these old scabby Rats, as it may prove injurious to the health of the dog.

It is surprising how far Rats will travel in the night. I have traced their tracks from a stackyard over two or three fields to a farm to get to their food. And you will always find that they have one time for feeding, which is as soon as it is dusk, the young Rats being the most venturesome for their food, always coming out first.

Rats, especially stackyard ones, are of a very clean nature. You will find that after they have had their first feed they diligently wash themselves. These Rats feed on nothing but good stuff, such as wheat, corn, and meal; and from experience I find that if a man is bitten on the hand by one of these Brown or Stack Rats it never "takes bad ways," but, if bitten by a dirty Drain Rat, then whether he cauterises or bathes the wound is no matter, it is sure to "take bad ways." I think the reason of this is because the Drain Rat, when it cannot get anything else to eat, exists on the worms and slugs, and this, I think, causes the teeth to become more venomous. When bitten in this way blood poisoning is very likely to ensue. Indeed, you must understand that the teeth of a full-grown Rat are quite half-an-inch long, and the jaw is very strong, so that if you are bitten on the finger it is almost sure to penetrate to the bone. I have known a good many cases of blood poisoning through Rat-bites.

The damage Rats can do to property, commodities, &c., is almost incredible. I have had so many examples of this that I scarcely know which to submit as illustration. I think the worst case I have seen was where they gnawed a hole half way through a 2¼ inch lead pipe, and often I have known them to bite through a one-inch lead pipe. The worst damage is done when they get under the flag floors of cottage houses out of the drains. They scratch the soil from beneath the flags, which then sink, and the consequent stench from the drains is abominable, jeopardising the health of the tenants. I have seen a great many of these cases in the poorer parts of Manchester. The damage the Rats will do in the silk and similar trades, to the goods of merchants, or in the grocery business, is enormous, and not so much by reason of what they actually eat as by what they carry away, which is often ten times as much as they eat. I have often proved this when ferreting at a wholesale grocery warehouse. When we have taken up the boards between the laths and plaster we have found the ceiling almost full of lump sugar, nuts, candles, &c., which have been there for years, hoarded by the Rats. Now, this all means heavy loss, and that is why I say that any business man so suffering ought to enage the services of a professional Rat-catcher once a year in order to keep the Rats down, and catch as many as possible before they begin breeding.

Another Rat habit may be noticed where the Rodents are accustomed to have their holes and runs among flags and stones. If they find any soft wood such as pine or white deal, they will nibble at it until it is eaten through. I have often known them to eat right through the legs of tables in the middle of cooking kitchens. This, I think, they do simply to keep their teeth clean and in order; I have known half-grown Rats to do the same.

Rats can exist a long time on herbage, if if they can get nothing more palatable. It is a very common thing to find Rats in the rabbit burrows when ferreting; in fact, I have seen, not once, but many times, Rats, rabbits, and weasels all bolt from the same burrow. I have also unearthed a Rat and a rabbit together out of one single burrow.

Now as to keeping Rats in store cages at home. Look well after them, and I think it is possible to keep them alive for quite a year; but if you keep, say, 20 in one store cage and neglect their feeding, you will find that when hungry in the night they will kill the weakest of their number and eat it, sometimes even eating two or three in one night, leaving the skin as clean as if a man had skinned them. It is always the best plan to put the Rats in different cages, according to their sizes. The young ones together, the old ones together, and the middle-aged ones together, as they keep themselves much cleaner when thus divided, and do not fight so much as they would otherwise. They must also be kept in a warm place; if not, they soon have cramp. Also keep them in a dark place and see that they have plenty of water; sprinkle them now and then with it so that they will wash themselves. It is astonishing what a hungry Rat will do. I I have seen them in the summer at dusk run at an old hen with her chickens under her, and almost as quick as I tell it, the Rat has snatched a live chicken and run with it under a pigsty floor.

I have known them to take half-grown young ducks from the water side. I remember once ferreting round a pit, near a barn, and when I put my ferret in the hole, it pulled out two dead chickens and three middle-sized dead ducks, and behind them, not more than a yard deep in the pit bank, was an old Rat. I have also known them to get into the coops where a gamekeeper was rearing his pheasants, and to kill nine young ones in a single night all from under the same hen.

Rats are also fond of eggs. I have read of many ways in which Rats take eggs, but in my quarter-of-a-century's experience of Ratting I never saw Rats take eggs save in one way, and that is, dragging or rolling them along the floor with their front paws, until they get them to the mouth of the hole. I remember one place where I was ferreting. There was an old cellar, the door of which at the top of the steps had to my knowledge been nailed up two or three years. Out of the hen house the Rats had eaten a hole at each side of the cellar door at the bottom. One day we burst open the door, went into the cellar (where it was impossible for a hen to get whilst the door was closed) and beneath the bottom step we caught two Rats. On lifting the flag at the bottom of the steps, we found 15 whole eggs, some good and some bad, all of which I am quite satisfied the Rats had carried down those nine stone steps! How they had done so I cannot explain, but content myself with stating only the plain facts of my own personal observation.

Rats are also very cunning in the water, say a pit or a river. Now, a Rat can exist in water for at most about seven minutes, and you will find when a dog is swimming after a Rat that the Rat is watching the dog all the time, for as soon as the dog gets within a yard of the Rat the latter will dive under water and come to the surface again about 15 yards away. When the dog has tired the Rat out with swimming, you will very often see the Rat dive again and come up very quietly and just put its nose out of the water, or rest its head on a floating leaf. It is so cunning that it will remain still there, and if the leaf or reed gives way it will come up at the water side and just thrust out its nose to breathe. By this means the dog loses full scent of the Rat.

I have also noticed how useful are the Rat's front paws and tail. I have seen a Rat on the top of a swill tub at a pigsty when the swill has been about ten inches from the top of the tub. The Rat was too cunning to jump down on the wet swill and drown, but I saw it reach as far down the inside of the tub as possible with its front paws and scrape the grease from around the sides! I have also seen the same Rat, when unable to scrape any further down the tub sides, turn round, clutch the top of the tub with its front paws, dip its tail into the swill, and then gain the top of the tub and commence licking its tail!

I have also tried an experiment with the same tub, which consisted of covering the top of the wet swill with bran, which floated on the surface, and placing a bit of lumpy swill in the middle of the bran, in the hope that the Rat would jump on the bran in the expectation of getting at the swill in the middle. However, it did not do so, no doubt instinctively guided against the danger.

I have also watched Rats run round a set wire or cage trap for a full hour. I have seen them go half way in and out again, look at the bait and never touch it, but go away and never return to the same trap that night. These examples show the cunning instinct of Rats.

There is, however, one power that the Rat is not favoured with, and I am afraid if they were they would be a greater pest. It is the ability of high jumping. A Rat cannot, I think, jump higher than three feet six inches, and will have to be very hungry before doing that to obtain food.

Many people may not know how fierce Rats are when fighting. Let me instance. I have often taken, one in each hand, two good Rats from my cage before a hundred spectators and set the Rats at each other on the top of a table. To see them fight would be surprising. They will fight like two bulldogs. When they have got a grip of each other with their teeth I have taken away my hands, and they have stuck and shook one another for at least half-a-minute, although you must understand that the moment they are loose of one another they are off if you don't catch them again.

There are several other cunning ways of Rats which I can scarcely explain. One must be amongst them regularly to know their wonderful ways and habits. Yet another little incident, in conclusion, may be of interest. I once called at a farm where they had been threshing a wheat stack. A Rat-catcher. had been there but without a dog, and when I arrived two hours afterwards my dog made a set, and commenced scratching amongst the old chaff left at the bottom of the stack, and to the astonishment of myself and the farmer

I pulled out of the hole where the dog was scratching 73 live Rats! The other Rat-catcher, who had been at the threshing all day, had caught only 14 Rats. This will serve to show that a Rat-catcher must not be without a good dog.

And now, respecting the ways and habits of Rats I think I have given my readers interesting and varied illustrations of what I have seen and experienced during my time.

PART IV.

—

LIFE OF THE RAT-CATCHER.

THIS work will not be complete if I do not deal with the Rat-catcher's life. The profession is a peculiar and exciting one, but all right if pursued in the right way. Although the calling takes one into dirty and obnoxious places, there is no reason why the Rat-catcher should not always appear respectable. The Rat-catcher has many temptations to dishonest conduct, for instance, when Rat-catching on a farm or private estate where there are numerous rabbits and game. It looks rather hard lines for the Rat-catcher to come off a farm with his cage full of Rats and see rabbits running about whilst he has all the requisites in his possession for catching them; and yet he must not touch one, but go home and merely reflect on what a good Sunday's dinner he is leaving behind. This I have experienced many a time, but I have always found even from the business view-point that the old

advice still remains true, " Honesty is the best
policy." Leaving the rabbits to themselves
has always turned out to be the best, for to
take a rabbit worth a shilling, and get caught
in the act, means that you can never go on
the same estate again. And from that same
estate you might have got 500 Rats in a year,
worth four shillings a dozen.

I must also put in a good word here for the
gamekeepers. My opinion is that if you go
on a keeper's ground and do what is right, you
will be able to go again, for in the whole of my
experience never having carried any nets but
Rat nets when on private estates, I have the
consolation of knowing that I should always
be welcome on going again to such estates.

Of course there are inconveniences that the
Rat-catcher has to put up with. Whatever
engagements he takes in a town, the only time
he can catch Rats with a good result is in the
night. On one occasion, when going round
with my bull's-eye lamp to examine the traps,
I was taken for a burglar by the policeman on
the beat, and he doubted me so much that he
would not release me until I had shown him
my cage with Rats in and my traps set all
over the place. Then he took almost as much
interest in the catching of Rats as myself, and
also brought in the other policemen who were

outside waiting for me to attempt an escape. Ever after that, when I had a night's engagement in any town, I always went to the police station to tell the man on that beat where I was.

It behoves the Rat-catcher to be always attentive to his customers, those, I mean, who want live Rats wherewith to try their dogs. Amongst mine I have the honour to include clients of highest rank and position, barristers, magistrates, solicitors and a host of sporting gentry. If the Rat-catcher's efforts commend themselves to such gentlemen, and he always maintains a respectable appearance, he will obtain some very nice outings in the country. Oft-times a party of gentlemen have sent for me in the summer, having arranged with me to bring four or five ferrets and Ratting appliances, and we have gone 50 miles up the country. They would bring their terrier dogs, and we would hunt all along the brooks and rivers, and round the corn and wheat fields, putting the Rats we caught into the cage, and after lunch, taking the Rats to a meadow and coursing them with their dogs, which I think it real good sport. We would put up at the best hotels and repeat the procedure next day, very often taking a drag or coach, and driving ten or a dozen miles farther up the country.

I can assure my readers that the Rat-catcher
is well remunerated for the trouble he under-
takes in these cases, and moreover this is
the class of people he requires to fraternise
with.   There is always a plentiful supply of
" refreshments " on these outings, and I would
therefore advise the Rat-catcher not to
indulge too freely.

The foregoing is, of course, a brief sketch of
the pleasantest part of a Rat-catcher's life,
and to complete the picture I may as well
describe some of the other features, and the
way he has to rough it sometimes.   Well,
Rat-catchers are generally called upon to
supply Rats for the Rat coursings usually
held at beerhouses, &c., on Saturday after-
noons, which one often sees advertised.   Now,
if he binds himself to supply a coursing at a
certain date, the bills announcing the event
are printed and posted, all of which means
expense.   Then you are bound to secure the
live Rats, whatever be the weather.   In doing
this I always followed the threshing machine
to the bays and stacks.   (Anyone that catches
Rats regularly can tell by looking at the bays
or stacks whether there are many Rats in or
not.)   I remember many times when the men
have started threshing a bay of wheat in which
were a great many Rats, and by dark they

have threshed only half of the bay. At such times the Rat-catcher must not leave the remaining half, no, not for half-an-hour throughout the whole night, for if he does the Rats will run out. To stop the Rats from leaving, the Rat-catcher has to lie on the top of the bay or go about every thirty minutes and beat the bottom with sticks until daylight, in order to keep the Rats in. Then, after the machine re-starts, and the bottom of the bay is reached, the Rat-catcher will be well paid for his trouble, for he may get, say, 150 good Rats for the coursing, at six shillings per dozen. The reason I call them good coursing Rats is because they have not been handled, and that enables them to run well.

Now, when you go to these coursings (which are mostly in the colliery districts) you will find about 60 dogs entered. It is the Rat-catcher's business to measure and handicap the dogs, and a very unpleasant job it is. He has also to be the referee at these coursings, and if it is a "near thing" with two dogs running at one rat, and you decide to award the victory to a given one, then the owner of the other dog will probably accuse you of wrong-doing and favouritism. Then is the time the Rat-catcher has to be prepared to pull off his coat and start fighting before, perhaps, 500 spectators. This has often occurred with me. This, I can assure my readers, is what I call "roughing it."

Of course, what I have just related occurred a few years ago, but when the Muzzling Order came into force, the authorities practically stopped Rat coursing, for they would not let a dog run at a Rat unless the dog was muzzled. This was about the worst thing that the authorities could do for Manchester and district, for at that time I was supplying for coursings about 100 Rats per week, and at the same time sending 50 Rats a week into Yorkshire, and all the Rats I supplied were caught within 15 miles of Manchester. This in my opinion, speaks very bad of the Muzzling Order, which I think is nothing but a farce, for at the very time I was going ratting, dogs were muzzled in some parts of the country but not in others. My opinion of dog muzzling is, muzzle all or muzzle none.

You will see by what I have said respecting these coursings, &c., that the Rat-catcher has plenty of work to supply so many live rats, and he has also to mix with company high and low. He also sometimes experiences difficulties in travelling on the railway. I have often entered an empty third-class carriage, sent my dog under the seat, and put the Rat cage there also. The carriage would fill with passengers, and upon reaching my destination I would take from under the seat my cage full of live Rats, to the amusement of some and the disgust of others.

I have also entered a railway carriage with my cage of rats when there were passengers in, one or two of whom would generally object to live Rats being in the same compartment, and on enquiring of the railway officials, I have found that any one travelling with live Rats is expected to put them in the guard's van.

I have also had a few good customers in my business, one or two in particular. Gentlemen have often sent me post-cards instructing me to take six or twelve Rats to their residences. I would run them out on the lawn in front of the house with their dogs, and generally I have received good remuneration for my trouble. These are the customers who should be looked well after, for they are the sportsmen who do not consider expense, though of course there are others who are just the opposite.

Further, Rat-catching is a business in which one is not called upon to allow credit. It is all a ready-money trade, and as there is not much competition, the Rat-catcher can command a good price for his work. He has always one resource open to him when he has

E

finished a job according to contract (catching say 40 or 50 Rats), should there be a dispute about the price and the people decline to pay the bill, then he has the expedient of letting the Rats at liberty again in the place where he had caught them. Most people will pay the price you send in rather than have the Rats turned loose again.

Although I am showing how the Rat-catcher can always have the advantage of stubborn payers, I may as well assure my readers that in all my experience such an occurrence as the above has never happened with me, simply because I always make my arrangements beforehand, which course I always find the best and most satisfactory all round.

Another matter I may mention. If any one could find out a sure way of catching Rats so that he could give a guarantee to clear large buildings, my opinion is that he would make a fortune in a very short time ; for I know firms in Manchester alone that would pay almost any amount to be rid of the Rats; not only because of what they consume, but more for the damage they do to their goods.

I have referred to the Rat-catcher obtaining good pay. The reason he commands such a big price for his work at the present time is because there is not much sale for live Rats.

The trade is not what it was some years ago when Rat-pits were allowed. I think it was one of the worst things they ever did for this country when the authorities stopped the Rat pits, for when Rat killing was allowed in pits, it was a common thing for a Rat-catcher to recieve an order for 100 Rats, all to be killed at one time; then the Rat-catcher would get the Rats and wherever he got them from he was ridding that district of a nuisance. But when the authorities stopped Rat-pits and Rat-coursing, the consequence was that the Rat-catcher left the Rats to breed in thousands. Rats being vermin, I don't see why they should not be killed 50 or 100 at a time in the pit, but the Humane Society maintain that it is cruelty to dogs to put them in a pit with a lot of Rats. I don't see where the cruelty comes in, but from what I have seen of Rat-pits during my time I approve of them, and I think if they were in existence again there would be a clearing of many thousands of Rats. Some 15 or 20 years since, I supplied 400 Rats in one week, all to be killed in Rat-pits.

Many of my readers may not understand what a Rat-pit is, and so I will just give an outline as well as I can.

The Rat-pit is of circular construction, say ten feet diameter, and about four feet six inches deep, the sides being perfectly smooth to prevent the rats climbing up and making their escape. A certain number of Rats are placed in the pit according to the arrangements made with the owner of the dog. Then the dog is put in the pit with the Rats to kill them, which a good dog does very quickly.

The reason the pit is built circular is so that the Rats will keep running round, for if it were square they would all run in a corner, one on the other, and then the dog would have no difficulty in killing them. It is better to have the pit fairly deep; if not, the rats might escape.

I think the best dog, within my recollection, that I have seen was a bull and fox terrier, which killed 40 good Rats in three minutes and 21 seconds. I have read and heard of dogs doing better feats, but I am only writing of what I have myself seen. I may say that the records for Rat-killing in Rat-pits are held by a dog called Jacko, which killed 200 Rats in 14 minutes and 37 seconds, and 1,000 Rats in less than one hour and 40 minutes.

The Rat-catcher has also some very dirty jobs to do sometimes. Often he has to go under all sorts of cellar floors, both wet and dry, but the majority of places are very wet and dirty, for the Rats nearly always come out of some filthy drain, and very often near a water-closet, the abominable smell arising from these places being sufficient to cause a fever.

I remember being once employed at a hospital, and I was paid at the rate of 5s. per visit for trapping Rats. Well, I found that 5s. per visit did not pay me (I had about 120 traps set all over the place), so I went before the committee and requested 8s. per night. The committee said they thought 5s. per visit was enough, and one or two of them said they thought 8s. per night was above a Rat-catcher's pay. Now, as I was not depending on that particular job at the time, I turned round and told them what I thought. I told them I considered Rat-catching was a skilled occupation, and I also offered any of them a five-pound note if they would only follow me under the floors at midnight, not to speak of taking the live Rats out of the traps in the dark; but I can assure you that none of these gentlemen would venture to undertake the task.

Now, if any of these gentlemen had to do this a few times they would not refuse to pay the Rat-catcher the sum he asks, viz., 8s. per night.

I remember more than once in big places

such as bonding warehouses, when I have been under the floors, my candle or lamp has gone out through being knocked over with grabbing at Rats, and I have not had a match in my pocket, and have had to grope about in the dark trying to find the trap-door where I have got under the floors, more often than not putting my hand in a set trap. It would be of no use shouting for a light simply because I have been alone. It is always better for a Rat-catcher to have assistance for night work, but I have done it myself very often.

Now, the expenses of travelling come very heavy sometimes, for wherever the Rat-catcher goes he always has to pay railway fare for himself and his dog.

Another thing I must tell you. Often when I have gone to inspect a small building I have found that there were a great many Rats in, but I have also known, after inspecting the place, that they have all come from the one place, out of the drain. Well, if I have contracted to do this job for a lump sum, I could easily clear this place and not catch an odd Rat, simply by ferreting them all back into the sewer in the daytime, and then making it good; but in most of these cases they do not like to pay your bill because you have caught no Rats. Still, you have driven them all down the drains, and after making the drain good they cannot get back again into the building.

Now, in a case like this I always trap them two or three nights and catch a few, just to give satisfaction to those engaging me.

Sometimes gentlemen will write inviting me to meet them at a certain farm, and bring my ferrets and a good supply of nets, alleging that there are "hundreds of Rats in the stacks." I just relate this to indicate how anyone not regularly amongst Rats can easily be deceived as to their numbers, for a couple of Rats on the thatch of a stack, especially when they have young ones, will probably have twelve holes eaten in the thatch and underneath the stack, and anyone not understanding their habits would think there were a lot of Rats in it.

And it is much the same with workpeople; if they chance to see two or three Rats at once, they will say there are "scores" of them. You would also be surprised to see the awful dread that tenants have of the Rat-catcher in private houses. When ferreting these places they think that if a Rat-catcher has once put his ferrets under the floor they will never see another Rat in the place; but depend upon it they are very bad to catch in these places.

I have often had much trouble respecting houses, warehouses, &c., to know whose duty it would be to pay the Rat-catcher for his work, the landlord's or the tenant's, but I think that the landlord should pay. I have had many engagements to catch Rats in newly-built houses before they were tenanted. The time the Rats get into these places is whilst the workmen are putting the drains in the back yards, leaving the drains open at nights. Thence the Rats come out and get under the floors, sometimes having to stop there, too, simply because the next day the joiners board up the floors and thus block the Rats in underneath, and then the Rats can always get into the kitchens up the back of the fireplace. Most property owners would do well to take note of this fact.

I must tell my readers, especially those having large shops, &c., that it is a good plan, if possible, to turn off the gas and water every night and week-end, for I have seen a good many cases where the Rats in the night-time have eaten through a water-pipe, and the place has been flooded by morning. It is just the same with a gas-pipe, and my opinion is that it is quite possible for fires to be caused by Rats in the night-time. Rats are very fond of nibbling and scratching at soft wood, and it would be an easy matter at a grocer's shop for a Rat to bite or scratch through the package of a gross of matches and ignite them, and the same cause may prove disastrous with any other inflammable goods.

Respecting the conveyance of live Rats, the Rat-catcher should always be particular to have good strong cages and bags, because if he had a number of Rats in an unserviceable bag which happened to break open at a railway station or in the street, I think he could be summoned for the damage the escaped Rats might do. Still, I have not in my time had or heard of a case of this sort.

Speaking of bags, a good many people seem to think that if a man puts his hand into a bagful of Rats they will bite him, but I can assure you that a child could do the same thing and not be bitten. Should there be only two or three in the bag, then they will bite, but not in the event of there being a good number. The same rule applies to Rats stored in a cage, where there is open daylight—if there be 40 or 50 Rats together, it is then the habit of the Rats for all to cling together, and they will let you handle them anyway if only you will have sufficient courage.

It is very good sport for gentlemen who want a good day's outing to go to farms when threshing is on, and also to go hunting and ferreting round the corn and wheat fields, and I think many sporting gentlemen who have not seen such sport would indulge in it freely after they had once witnessed it. I think it is much better and healthier sport than rabbit-shooting, especially in the summer when the farmers are cutting their corn and wheat.

When catching Rats as a regular pursuit, one is surprised at the queer places in which he finds them. I recollect ferreting seven full-sized Rats from under the floor of a built dog kennel not above four yards square, where a large mastiff and a terrier dog slept every night, only a ¾-inch board dividing them from the Rats, and the Rats having eaten holes through the boards in the kennel! I have also found at an out-house an old bitch Rat and nine young ones in an old tin trunk without a lid. I have also caught Rats and taken young ones out of the nest from under railway sleepers where trains have been running and shunting operations carried on every day. And I have even taken old and young ones in their nest from a pile of Cheshire cheese, at a wholesale cheese and bacon factor's!

And mentioning cheese in this connection reminds me that once I discovered that Rats had scratched and eaten a hole direct through the bottom lot of cheese in a pile which had only been there three weeks.

A word or two about what a Rat will do with a ferret. I have often seen a Rat run a ferret out of the hole, and then wait with its head out of the hole until the ferret has come to it again. I remember once ferreting at a hencote, and put the ferret behind the hen nest, whereupon the Rat attacked the ferret, which then jumped back and died in five minutes, the Rats having given only one bite behind the ferret's ear! Of course this is a very rare occurrence. True, I have had many ferrets killed by Rats in my time, but it has always occurred through the poisonous bite first swelling and then "taking bad ways," the ferret dying in probably a week or so.

You must understand that if you put a Rat and a ferret together in a tub the ferret would kill the Rat in nine cases out of ten, the nature of the Rat being to get away from the ferret if possible; but if it cannot it will fight, and I think a Rat, for its size, is of a very vicious nature, for I have often seen when trying a puppy at killing a Rat in a pit, that a game Rat will run the puppy all round the pit. The best way to try a pup to kill a Rat is to draw the teeth of the first Rat it secures for sometimes if a pup gets a severe bite from a Rat it will never look at another. It is a very bad plan to let a pup play with a Rat too much, for this causes the pup never to put a hard mouth on the Rat. When this latter occurs it is the best plan not to allow the same pup to see another Rat until it is a month or two older. If you will take care and trouble with a pup you can bring it up to your own liking, and to do anything you want. I have worked seven years with a curly-coated retriever bitch, and when ferreting a brook she would stand in the water and catch the Rats that escaped from the nets into the brook and bring them to me alive in her mouth. I have sold hundreds of Rats she has caught in this manner, and to show you how the dogs can be brought up with the ferrets I need only mention that this bitch would lie down and let two ferrets kill a Rat on the curly coat of her back.

Farmers know too well of the many restless nights the cows and horses experience through Rats. I have seen when trapping all night at a farm the Rats running over the cows and horses whilst sleeping: and when horses have been working in the field all day they want better rest in the night. I have known when farmers would not let the Rat-catcher ferret their buildings gratis, simply because they have a few hens sitting. They don't consider that when the hens have hatched the eggs the Rats will take the chickens. Whenever a farmer has refused to let me ferret at his farm I have passed that farm ever afterwards. To show you the different dispositions of farmers I have met, I may mention that when once ferreting at a farm, we caught nine rats and lost the ferret, and two days afterwards the ferret was found on the farm, and I sent for it, but the farmer demanded two shillings of me for the ferret's keep. This same man I may add farmed about two hundred acres.

Of course, there are other farmers just the opposite, who will not only pay you for your trouble, but take great interest in helping you to catch the Rats. I relate these facts and incidents to show you the contrast in the disposition of different people one meets in this business.

I don't think the Rat-catcher's life is one of the worst if he looks well after his business, for he has a few advantages over other occupations. In the first place, he is his own master, and need only doff his coat when he chooses, there being for him no such summons to work as a factory bell. And if he fancies a day's outing in the country he can always take his dog and ferrets with him, and make a day's pleasure into a remunerative business, by reason of the income from the Rats, and I find from experience that the best friends he has are his dog and ferrets, if he will look well after them and treat them kindly, for I think that a Rat-catcher in the country without a good dog might walk over scores of Rats and never know they were there, so you will see that his dog is chiefly what he has to trust to.

And now, in conclusion, let me express the hope that this book will prove instructive, entertaining, and profitable to my readers, inasmuch as I have endeavoured to make it so to the best of my ability and within the somewhat limited scope and sphere of a Rat-catcher's calling. Of course, I might have made the narrative portion of the book more startling and exciting, had I drawn upon my imagination, but I have thought it best to adhere to cold fact and actual experience.

HINTS ON RABBIT SHOOTING.

Always have your gun made at your gun-maker's to your own liking.

Always be prepared for the worst of weather, and be sure to have good strong boots.

Never have your gun on full cock while walking about, especially whilst going through a fence.

Never stand too close to a burrow, and don't be too eager to shoot.

Always have your gun pointed upwards to the clouds or down to the ground.

Never shoot at a rabbit as it sits on the top of the hole, or you might shoot the ferret.

Always stand so that all the shooters can see one another.

Never remove from where the gamekeeper places you.

Never have your gun barrels up while it is raining.

When you go out in the country always provide yourself with refreshments before starting.

If you miss an easy shot don't blame the gun.

Don't be too excited, and get well on the rabbits before you pull.

If the keeper's dog is retrieving rabbits never attempt to take one from it.

IKE MATTHEWS is prepared to go out Ratting with parties of gentlemen or their gamekeepers on their private estates during the summer, supplying dog, ferrets, and nets, at moderate charges. Arrangements may be made by post.

IKE MATTHEWS is also willing to go out rabbit-shooting with gentlemen during the season, and will supply and work ferrets at reasonable charges. He is also prepared to break dogs and puppies to ferreting and Ratting on reasonable terms.

Any number of live Rats and rabbits supplied at a few days' notice.

All orders promptly attend to.

Undeniable References.

Yours truly,

IKE MATTHEWS.

www.ingramcontent.com/pod-product-compliance
Lightning Source LLC
Chambersburg PA
CBHW031243260626
47169CB00007B/2434